Fetch to the Rescue

Story by Stephen Thraves

Based on the TV series, Fetch the Vet

Little
Hippo

With thanks for technical help:
Suzanne Whight BVSc MRCVS
(Greenwood Veterinary Clinic, Chalfont St Peter)

Scholastic Children's Books,
Commonwealth House, 1-19 New Oxford Street,
London WC1A 1NU, UK
a division of Scholastic Ltd

London ~ New York ~ Toronto ~ Sydney ~ Auckland
Mexico City ~ New Delhi ~ Hong Kong

First published in the UK by Scholastic Ltd, 2000

Based upon the television series FETCH THE VET produced
by Flextech Rights Ltd and ITEL in association with Cosgrove Hall Films.
Original concept by Stephen Thraves and Gail Penston.

Text copyright © Stephen Thraves, 2000
Illustrations derived from FETCH THE VET television series,
copyright © Flextech Rights Ltd and ITEL, 2000.
Photographs by Jean-Marc Ferriere and Justin Nöe

ISBN 0 439 99732 1

Printed in Spain

Tom Fetch the vet was having a very busy morning at the Duckhurst Animal Clinic. He had examined rabbits, tortoises and guinea pigs. Now he was looking at George Moffatt's sheepdog, Mitch.

George was the farmer at Whitecliff Farm. He loved his animals and became very worried when one of them was poorly.

"So Fetch," said George nervously. "Will Mitch be all right again?"

"Of course he will, George," said Fetch. "It's only a small ear infection. I've got just the medicine for him."

Pippa and Lucy lived next door to the animal clinic. George Moffatt was their uncle. Pippa was quite worried when she saw his car outside the clinic.

"I hope there's nothing wrong with any of the animals," Pippa said to Lucy.

They both hurried round to the clinic to find out!

"I expect you've come to see Mitch," said Kara to Pippa and Lucy as they arrived at the clinic. "Why don't you sit and wait for him? He'll be out soon."

The girls sat down on the waiting room chairs.

"You want to be a vet one day, don't you, Pippa?" Lucy said.

"Sssh, Lucy," whispered Pippa, "that's supposed to be a special secret!"

The girls didn't have to wait long. Fetch and George soon came out of the surgery with Mitch.

"Look at Mitch!" laughed Lucy. "He's got a lampshade on his head!"

Fetch explained to the girls that it was a special collar to stop Mitch scratching his ear. He had to wear it until his ear was completely better.

"Can we go back to the farm with you and Mitch now, Uncle George?" said Pippa.

"Of course you can," said George. "You know you're always welcome. Let's go!"

When the girls arrived at the farm, they saw Joe, their cousin.

"Hello Pippa, hello Lucy," called Joe. "Will you help me find Trevor? He's run off again!"

Pippa giggled. Trevor the goat was always wandering off and getting lost!

"We've got to find Trevor," said Lucy firmly, "I want to play with him!"

They started looking for Trevor on the farm. Then suddenly, Mitch ran off . . .

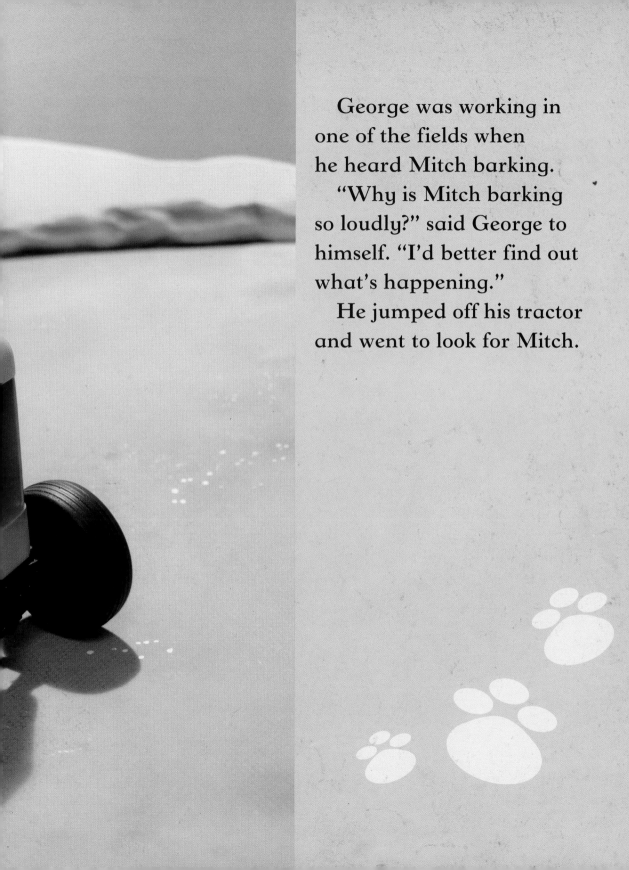

George was working in
one of the fields when
he heard Mitch barking.
  "Why is Mitch barking
so loudly?" said George to
himself. "I'd better find out
what's happening."
  He jumped off his tractor
and went to look for Mitch.

George found Mitch standing by the fence at the edge of the cliffs. Mitch was barking loudly,

"Woof, woof! Woof, woof!"

The children heard all the noise and hurried into the field towards George and Mitch.

"Stop right there!" George shouted to them. "It's very dangerous here!"

"What's happened, Uncle George?" asked Pippa.

"Trevor has fallen over the edge of the cliffs!" said George. "We have to help him as quickly as we can."

Luckily, Trevor had become tangled up in the fence and had not fallen very far. But the fence looked as if it would break at any moment.

"I must try to pull him up!" said George, as he reached down towards Trevor.

But George couldn't move Trevor – he was too tangled up in the fence. The more George pulled the fence, the more it cut into Trevor's leg.

"We can't just leave Trevor there!" said Joe. "We must think of something!"

Then Mitch started to bark. He was trying to tell them something. At first, no-one could work out what he meant, but then George realised what Mitch was saying.

"He's telling us to FETCH THE VET!" George cried. "Run and phone the clinic, Joe. Ask Mr Fetch to come right away!"

"Okay, Dad," said Joe and he ran off towards the farmhouse.

Back at the animal clinic, Fetch thought that his very busy morning was finally coming to an end. But he was wrong! At the last minute, another patient arrived.

It was Violet Blush!

"Oh, Mr Fetch. It's my darling Romeo!" sobbed Violet, as she put down her special cat basket. "He's got a terrible pain in his tummy!"

"Now, don't worry, Violet," said Fetch. "Let me take a look at him."

Fetch examined Romeo in his surgery, but as usual, he could find absolutely nothing wrong with him. The spoilt cat had just been eating too much food again!

Suddenly Kara ran quickly into the surgery.

"We've just had an emergency telephone call from Whitecliff Farm," she said. "George Moffatt's goat is trapped on the cliff edge! You have to go right away, Tom."

"Sorry, Violet," said Fetch. "I've got to go. I'll come and see you later on my rounds."

Fetch picked up his bag and ran out of the clinic. He jumped into his car and drove as quickly as he could to Whitecliff Farm. There wasn't a minute to lose!

When Fetch reached the farm, he ran across the fields.

"Mr Fetch is here, Dad," called Joe.

"Don't worry, George," said Fetch, as he reached the edge of the cliff. "Just hold on a few seconds longer!"

Fetch quickly took a special pair of cutters out of his bag and, with George's help, carefully cut Trevor free of the fence.

Then very slowly, and very gently, Fetch and George started to pull Trevor up.

"Nearly there, George!" panted Fetch, as Mitch and the children all watched anxiously. Finally, Trevor was back on the cliff top again!

"That was a lucky escape!" said Fetch, wiping his brow.

"Mr Fetch has rescued you, Trevor!" cried Pippa. "You're safe now!"

Lucy threw her arms around Trevor's neck and gave him a big hug.

"Well done, George," said Fetch, "you found Trevor just in time!"

"It was Mitch who found Trevor," said George proudly. "He's a clever old fellow, aren't you, Mitch?"

Mitch wagged his tail happily as everyone cheered.